Questions About Santa

Santa Claus A.K.A. Kris Kringle

How does Santa get in the house?

Does he make the Presents?

Does he Steal all the toys?

Is he an elf that raised other elves to make toys?

For my holiday cookies
Noah, Milo, Zen, and Lotus
and for my mom Katharyn
and my sister Nefeterius

www.theenglishschoolhouse.com
Text copyright © 2020 by Tamara Pizzoli
Pictures copyright © 2020 by Anna Angrick
ISBN: 978-0-9992108-1-9

The Claus Conspiracy

Written by Dr. Tamara Pizzoli
Illustrated by Anna Angrick

THE ENGLISH SCHOOL HOUSE

Spencer Stanford had been a skeptic for as long as he or anyone in his family could remember. He just wasn't the type of kid to accept things at face value.

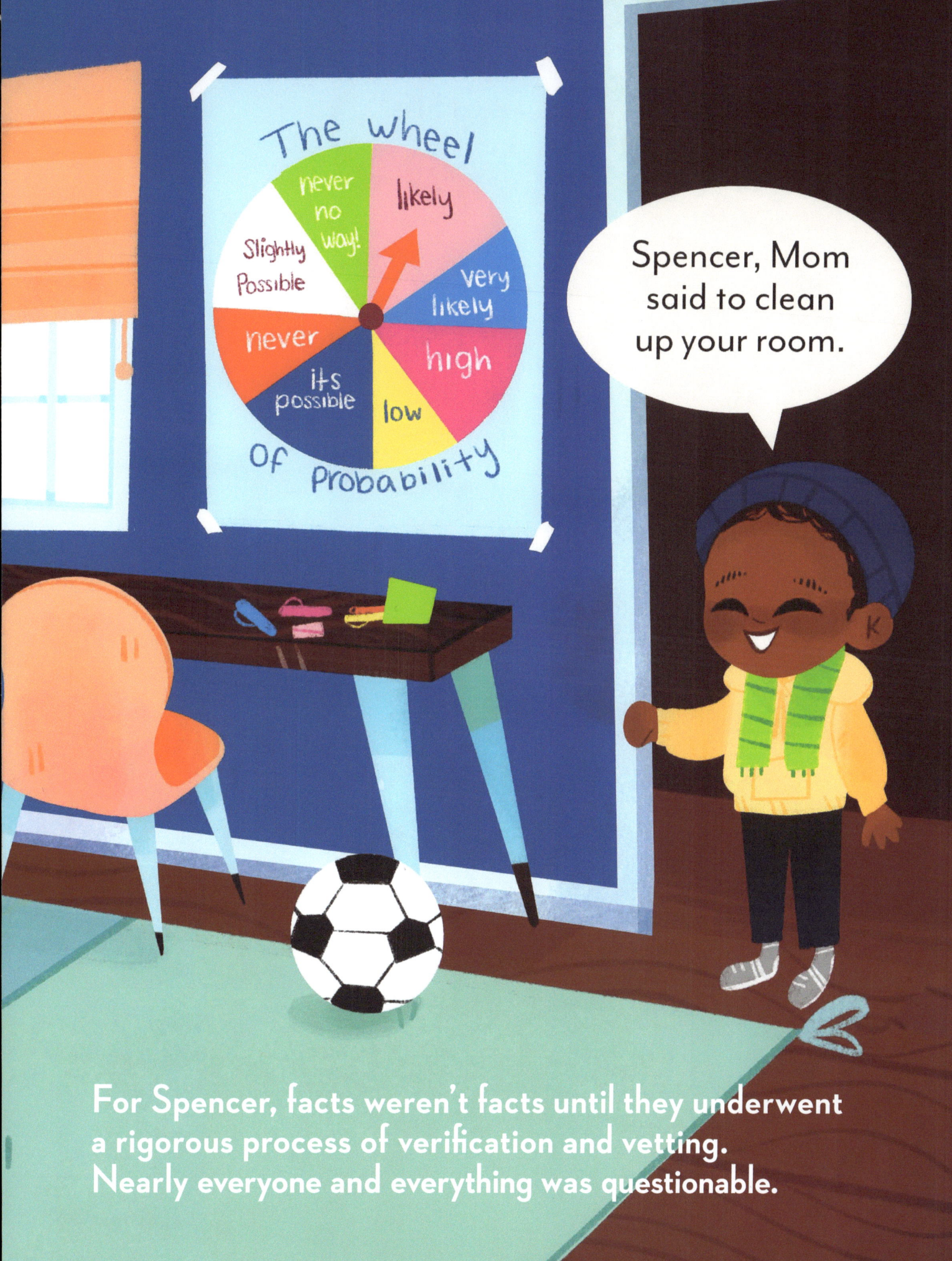

For Spencer, facts weren't facts until they underwent a rigorous process of verification and vetting. Nearly everyone and everything was questionable.

Spencer's family was used to his constant queries and supported his curiosity.

FROZEN

milk!

food town

milk

lactose free milk!

milk lactose free!

try it today!

But if it's milk, how can it be lactose free?

2 for 1!

Is this sale really two for one or is there a catch?

But even they had to admit his questions could suffer from bad timing.

No subject brought up more mixed feelings and seeds of doubt for Spencer than that of Santa Claus.

QUESTIONS ABOUT SANTA

How does Santa get in the house?

Santa Claus AKA Kris Kringle

Does he steal all the toys?

Does he make the presents?

Is Santa a big elf that raised other elves to make toys?

He wasn't the only one. Half of Spencer's friends had stopped believing in Santa altogether.

But for every dubious pal,
Spencer could count an equal
number of friends who were
firm believers.

Dear Santa,

My name is Spencer Stanford and I have some concerns I'd like to bring to your attention. I'm starting to think the idea that you bring presents to all of the kids around the world may be a big hoax. My main questions are as follows:

—If thats the case, why? What's in it for you?

—Is your beard real?

—Do you ever shave it?

—Are the mall Santas your cousins?

—How are all the presents made?

  —How do you get into houses without chimneys?

    —Are all the presents made at the North Pole?

    —Are you a big elf who's raised by smaller elves to make toys?

    —Do you steal the toys?

    I'd appreciate it if you'd answer my questions, and if you're real, I'd like proof please, or a sign.

        Sincerely,
        Spencer Stanford

One Tuesday afternoon in early December, Spencer decided to launch a proper investigation. He sat down at his desk and laid it all out in a detailed letter addressed to Santa.

Spencer mailed
the envelope
the very next day.

A few days later
it arrived at
111 Claus Place,
The North Pole.

Santa was relaxing in the den when his wife Charlene, just home from her shopping trip, brought in the mail.

Santa soon settled into his favorite chair and began to read aloud the daily letters:

"Dear Santa...I want a microscope..."
"Dear Santa...I want a bike..."

The contents of the third envelope, however, made him sit straight up in his Easy Guy Deluxe Chair with the multiple cookie holders.

"I don't believe this!" Santa griped in a huff.

"What is it?" Mrs. Claus shouted from the kitchen.

"This kid wants proof that I exist. And if that wasn't enough... he actually asked me in this letter if I steal the presents! The nerve!"

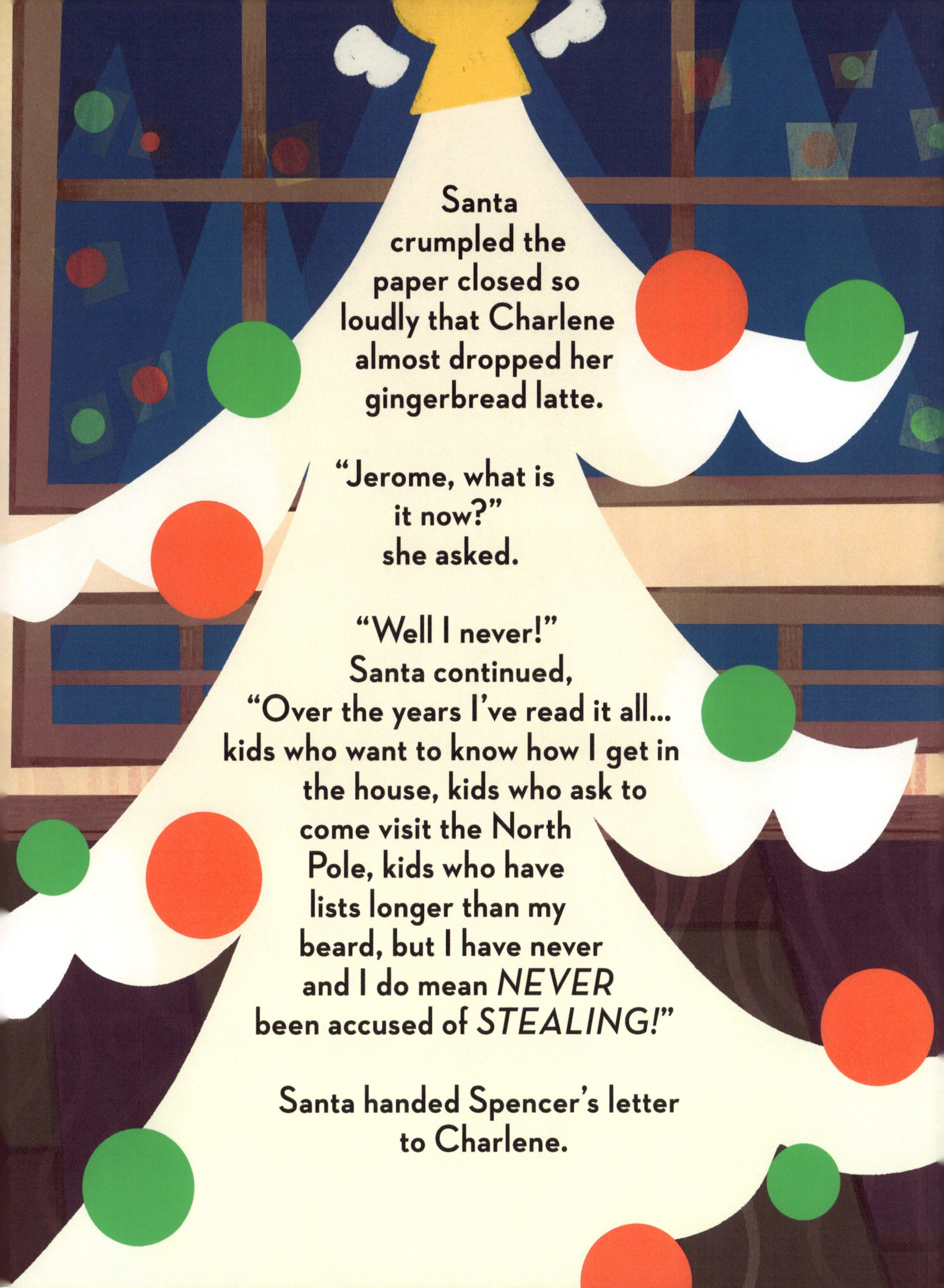

Santa crumpled the paper closed so loudly that Charlene almost dropped her gingerbread latte.

"Jerome, what is it now?" she asked.

"Well I never!" Santa continued, "Over the years I've read it all... kids who want to know how I get in the house, kids who ask to come visit the North Pole, kids who have lists longer than my beard, but I have never and I do mean *NEVER* been accused of *STEALING!*"

Santa handed Spencer's letter to Charlene.

"Well darling," Santa's wife began,
"I think it's normal that this child would like some clarification. Just think of how many children around the world have, well, different ideas about you than what's actually true—Like the children in Italy who think you're married to some witch.
I've never appreciated that. And in Sweden there's that gnome with the red hat and the goats, and then there's the mall Santa phenomenon.
That alone could confuse any kid."

Santa stroked his beard in deep thought.

Charlene continued, "I know it's your busy season, honey. But maybe it's time to set the record straight."

The Dallas Police Department has recieved a report that Tallulah the Tooth Fairy is possibly leaving fake money for children in exchange for teeth.

"I know!" Santa finally exclaimed. "I'll put out a press release! Better yet, I'll set up a televised interview. I'll contact that journalist over at Faux News, Lionne Painglin and ..."

"Oh no!" Charlene interrupted, "almost nothing that comes out of her mouth on that program is credible. There she is on the tv now spreading lies for ratings. I know Tallulah and she would never do something like this."

"No, Jerome," Charlene continued, "you need something bigger and completely reliable."

"But what?" Santa pondered aloud.

He tossed and turned all night considering what might be done.

Santa awoke early the next morning with a clearer idea of what steps to take next. He decided to ask some good friends for advice. As chairman of the Forefathers of Fairy Tales Council, Santa convened an emergency conference call.

All of the heavy hitters were present: The Easter Bunny, The Halloween Witch, Tallulah the Tooth Fairy and the newest member of the board, The Boogey Man.

"Alright, y'all. I'd like some input..."
Santa explained his dilemma in detail.

"I want to clear up some things for Spencer without ruining the magic of what we do here at the North Pole," he said.

"I welcome your suggestions on what to do."

By the next morning, Santa's chat inbox was full of recommendations.

WhatsThat Chats

Broadcast List   **New Groups**

Tallulah the Tooth Fairy CEO

I've been through something similar. Leave a note and explain yourself.

Boogeyman

He's a brat. Leave him coal.

Tituba the Halloween Witch

Just leave him candy. Kids forget everything when we get the sweet stuff.

Estelle the Easter Bunny

In the end, Jerome Nicholas Claus was grateful for his friends' advice, but decided to trust his first mind and make a bold statement that would be seen by the world.

Mom! Dad! It's magic! Santa got my letter!

Happy Holidays from Jerome Claus, Esq., The Real Santa

Coming soon: The Santa Connection Channel featuring Cooking with Santa Shows, Question and Answer sessions, virtual tours of our Toy Factory, updates on "Naughty or Nice" list statuses and more...

Dear Spencer Stanford,
I have never stolen a thing in my life. It's important to ask questions when you're unsure. I hope you like what we're dropping off for you this year.
Yours truly, Santa

As Spencer unwrapped his gifts on Christmas morning, he was certain that each one had been chosen and delivered with love and care.

I know they are.